Fern and Kate

Meet Samuel Coleridge-Taylor

By David Gleave

For Stuart, Jonathan and Rebecca

Another Feather for Fern

Fern and Kate were lined up with their class outside the Fairfield Halls in Croydon.

It was a hot day and Mrs Grainger kept counting and re-counting the children to make sure everyone was there. She must have counted at least three times and Fern was getting restless.

'I can't believe she's dragged us here to listen to "classical" music,' said Fern.

'I know,' said Kate 'this is going to be boring.'

'I'm bored already,' said Fern.

'What are you two whispering about?' Mrs Grainger asked, giving them her special "look".

'Nothing Miss,' the two girls said together.

'Right, we're going in now. Does anyone need the toilet before we start? Fern, do *you* need the toilet? I really don't want you wandering off again like you did when we visited Kenwood.'

'I'm fine, Miss,' and seeing Mrs Grainger looking at her suspiciously, she added 'really, I am fine.'

'Right, in we go then. In your pairs and please be quiet, most of the other schools will already be here.'

They filed into the hall. It was big, Fern had never been in a hall this big before. It made their "hall" at school where they did whole school assemblies seem tiny by comparison.

Most of the seats were already full and Fern thought everyone had turned to stare at them as they came in although really only a few children had. She noticed one boy sitting right up at the back of the hall, he was dressed a bit strangely and he was sitting all by himself. She felt a bit sorry for him. She pointed him out to Kate by nodding in his direction. 'Special,' Kate whispered.

The lights went down, the musicians came out on stage and everyone settled down. The music started. Kate had been right, this *was* boring, not an electric guitar in sight.

Fern kept glancing over her shoulder at the boy at the back of the hall. He was waving his arms around as if he was conducting the music. Fern nudged Kate and nodded in his direction.

'See,' whispered Kate 'I told you he was special.'

'I'm going to talk to him, just because he's special doesn't mean we should ignore him, look, he's all by himself, I feel sorry for him.'

'Please don't,' Kate begged but it was too late, Fern had slipped out of her seat and was creeping up the steps towards the back of the hall. Normally Mrs Grainger wouldn't have let Fern sit on the end of a row because she liked to keep an eye on her but they had arrived late and she had been a bit flustered.

Fern was able to get to the boy without anyone noticing. 'Hello,' she said quietly 'would you like to come and sit with us?'

He looked at her, a bit confused, but smiled and said 'no thank you, I've got a really good view from here and there are no distractions from the music. Or there *weren't* any.'

'Sorry,' said Fern, a little bit hurt, 'I thought you looked a bit lonely up here by yourself.'

'Oh, it's OK,' he said 'I didn't mean to be rude. My name's Samuel, Sam for short. Some people call me "Sambo".'

Fern winced 'that isn't very nice, that's racist, isn't it?' She wasn't sure but she thought it probably was.

'I don't know,' said Sam 'they usually smile and ruffle my hair as they say it.'

'I'm not sure that makes it any better,' said Fern. 'My name's Fern, I'm here with my school.'

'What do you think of the music?'

'It's really boring.' Seeing the look of horror on his face she added 'it isn't really my thing, I prefer electric guitars.'

'I've never heard of an "electric" guitar, that sounds very odd. What sort of sound do they make?'

'All sorts, mwaaaaa, mwaaaaa, waaaaaa, waaaaaa,' she did her best but it was an odd question.

'Well that doesn't sound like my thing,' he said, laughing softly. 'I hope you enjoy the second half more, they're going to perform one of my pieces, though I haven't written it yet.'

He really is "special" she thought but he seemed harmless. 'I don't understand how anyone can perform it if it hasn't been written yet.'

'No, it's a puzzle isn't it?' He chuckled at some private joke. 'It's called "Hiawatha's Wedding Feast".'

'A wedding? I like the sound of that.'

'It's based on a poem.'

'I like poetry, well some of it anyway.'

'I set it to music.'

'Except you haven't yet.'

'That's right, but I will do. It's going to be a huge success and make me very famous.' Fern looked doubtful, very doubtful. 'You'll see,' he added.

Suddenly Kate appeared beside them. 'Fern, you'd better come back, I think the first half is about to end and when the lights go on, Miss is bound to spot you.'

'I'm just talking to …' but before she could finish her sentence Mrs Grainger was looming over them in the semi-darkness.

'Right, Fern, I've had just about enough of you wandering off, back to your seat immediately. I'm going to be watching you like a hawk from now on.'

'Sorry Miss, but I was just talking to Samuel here and he said …' She turned but there was no sign of Samuel, he had vanished. She turned back to Mrs Grainger 'there was a boy here and I was talking to him. His name was Samuel and he said he wrote some of the music in the second half.'

'Oh Fern you must stop making things up.' The lights had gone up now and Fern could see that Mrs Grainger looked angry and concerned at the same time.

'It's true Miss,' Fern felt as if she was going to cry but knew she mustn't. 'It was something to do with a wedding.'

'"Hiawatha's Wedding Feast"?'

'That's it, yes Miss. He said he wrote that. That he was going to write it anyway.' Even Fern could hear how ridiculous this sounded.

'"Hiawatha's Wedding Feast" was written by Samuel Coleridge-Taylor…'

'You see, he said his name was Samuel!'

'… who died over a hundred years ago,' Fern looked crestfallen 'so you see, Fern,' Mrs Grainger said gently 'you can't possibly have met him, it was probably just someone playing a silly trick.'

Fern stood up to go but as she did so she felt something under her hand. She looked down and picked up … a feather. Mrs Grainger saw it. 'Where did you get that, Fern?'

'I don't know Miss, it was just there' she hesitated 'perhaps Samuel dropped it.'

Mrs Grainger frowned and tutted and said 'it's probably from one of the headdresses, they're going to do the "Wedding Feast" in full costume so it probably got dropped after a dress rehearsal.'

Fern found the second half of the concert much more fun. She really enjoyed the Wedding Feast, the words told an interesting story and the music was exciting. There were people dressed up and they stomped around a wigwam in time with the music.

'Thanks for bringing us, Miss,' Fern said as they filed out of the hall. Mrs Grainger was counting again, she always seemed to be counting.

Mrs Grainger gave her an odd look. 'I'm glad you enjoyed it, Fern.'

'What do you know about Samuel, Miss?'

'Samuel?'

'Yes Miss, the boy, man, who wrote the music.'

'Oh right, well I know that he was mixed race, sorry, mixed heritage like you, Fern,' Mrs

Grainger corrected herself, it was so hard to keep up with the correct way of describing people like Fern 'and that he lived not far from here. But instead of me just telling you about him why don't you see what you can find out for yourself. Perhaps there are some books in the library at school.' Noticing the look on Fern's face she added 'but you aren't much of a one for books are you, Fern? Why not see what you can find out about him on the internet?'

That sounded more like fun, she could do that in her bedroom at home.

'I will, Miss, and can I do "show and tell" next Friday? I could show people this feather.' She held it up.

'Well it's certainly a very nice feather but let's see how you get on shall we?' She looked closely at Fern's face 'I wish you were always this interested in your school work, Fern.'

'I want to find out about …' She was going to say "the boy I met" but knew Mrs Grainger still didn't believe her so instead she said 'the man who wrote the "Wedding Feast" music because I really enjoyed it.'

'That's very good Fern, now let's get on the coach with the others.'

As they left the building, Fern noticed a small sign on the wall about Samuel Coleridge-Taylor.

She was going to point it out to Mrs Grainger but she was too busy counting, again.

*

'Fern!' Fern's Mother was calling up the stairs to her. 'What are you doing up there?'

'Homework Mum,' said Fern, appearing at the top of the stairs.

'Well come down, your tea's ready.'

Fern scampered down the stairs, she was starving. She'd been doing a lot of research on the internet and had found out a lot about Samuel Coleridge-Taylor but had completely lost track of the time.

'I really don't know what I was thinking when I agreed to let you have a computer in your room, you're far too young and you seem to spend most of your time up there.' Actually Mrs Green knew exactly why she had agreed, it was a treat to make up for Fern's Dad not being around, but it had surely been a mistake.

'It's really useful for school work, Mum, I don't know how I managed without one.'

Fern sat in front of the telly with a tray balanced on her knees, eating the food her Mother had prepared.

'Don't forget I'm going out later, I'll be back by eight. What's this homework you've been so busy with?'

'You remember I told you about the concert I went to?' Her Mother nodded. 'Well I've been finding out about the man who composed some of the music.'

'That's nice.'

'He was mixed race and he was very famous about a hundred years ago.'

'Uh huh.' Fern could tell her Mother wasn't really listening.

'Mum, can we go and look at the house where he lived? It isn't far.'

'We'll see.'

'You always say that but you never really mean it. "We'll see" usually means "no".'

'I'm very busy, Fern. Since your Father left I've had to take on extra work, you know that.'

'But you don't work on Saturdays Mum. Please. It's school work.'

'OK, we'll fit it in if we can. Now, I really must get ready to go out. I've arranged for someone to pop round and keep an eye on you.'

'Oh Mum, I'm perfectly capable of looking after myself for a couple of hours, I am *eight* you know.'

'It's Femi's Mum.'

'Oh, that's different, I really like her. Do you think she'd do my hair?' Fern held up a knotted clump as if her Mum might need reminding what hair was. 'She's …' Fern was going to say "she's better at it than you" but knew that would sound rude 'she won't mind, will she?'

'If you ask her nicely I expect she might do it.'

'She tells lovely stories about her own country.'

'As far as I know she's lived here for over thirty years, I'd have thought this was her "own country" as you put it,' Fern's Mum said a bit grumpily.

'I don't suppose you ever forget where you were born. Didn't Dad always say "remember your roots, Fern"?'

'Yes, well your Father said lots of things but let's not talk about him now. I'll see you later. I'll be back before you go to bed.'

Fern went back to her room, there was lots more to find out about Samuel Coleridge-Taylor.

*

Fern had persuaded her Mother to take her and Kate to see the house in South Norwood where Samuel Coleridge-Taylor used to live.

'What do you want to go there for?' her Mother had asked 'It's just going to be a house like any other.'

'It's for my school project, the one I'm doing for Mrs Grainger, I need a photo.' Fern knew that words like "school" and "project" worked well in situations like this. Things that might otherwise have got a straight "no" or a "maybe" could be turned into a "yes" if you made it sound like school work.

'I still don't really understand but we can get a bus straight there so it shouldn't take too long.'

Now they were here, walking down Dagnall Park Road, looking for number 30, she was excited. Kate was just glad to be out of her house, her parents had been arguing a lot recently and she was fed up with it. Fern's Mum didn't seem to have that problem anymore and, as far as Kate could see, she was happier for it. She never mentioned this to Fern who she knew was still upset by her Father's absence.

They were almost there when Fern's Mother stopped 'Hello Peggy,' she said to a woman working in the front garden of one of the houses.

'Hello,' the woman said 'what brings you here?'

'We're going to see a house where some composer used to live.'

'That'll be number 30, there's a plaque on the wall, though I can't remember what it says. It's only two doors down, you can't miss it.'

'It's been a while hasn't it, Peggy?'

'It has, I heard you've had a bit of trouble with …' Peggy looked anxiously in the direction of the girls 'you know.'

'Yes. I most certainly did.'

Fern could tell that her Mother was going to get into a long discussion about her Father that she didn't particularly want to hear and she was anxious to get to the house they'd come to see. She gave her Mother's arm a little bit of a tug.

'Why don't you two girls go ahead and take your picture while I chat to Mrs Wellard? Come straight back when you've finished. It's only two doors you say?' she asked Peggy.

'That's right, they'll be fine.'

So Fern said 'see you in a minute,' and she and Kate carried on down the road.

Peggy had been right, there was no chance of missing the house as it had a blue sign on the front wall

Fern read the words 'Samuel Coleridge Taylor, 1875 to 1912, composer of The Song of Hiawatha, lived here.' Then she took a photo of the house and then one of Kate with the house behind her. Then Kate took a picture with Fern in it. It only took a minute.

'Mum was right,' Fern said 'it isn't anything very special, just an ordinary old house. If it wasn't for the sign you wouldn't know there was anything different about it at all.' Kate agreed but she still thought it was better than being cooped up in the house with her parents.

They were about to go back to Fern's Mother when Fern suddenly had a strong feeling that they were being watched. She was sure there was someone hiding behind the hedge in the garden. She shouldn't have done it but, without thinking, she picked up a small pebble from the path and tossed it into the hedge.

'Hey, what did you do that for, you nearly hit me?' It was a boy's voice. She was pretty sure it was Sam's voice. The boy stepped out into the open and, sure enough, it was the boy she'd seen at Fairfield Halls, it was Sam!

'What are you doing here?' she asked at exactly the same moment he was asking her the same question. They laughed.

'Well I'm going to live here when I grow up,' he said proudly.

'And I came because this is a house I know that you did live in.'

'Hang on a minute,' said Kate 'how can he, I mean how can you, possibly know you are going to live here in the future. Don't you mean you live here now?'

'It's strange isn't it,' said Fern and Sam in unison 'he just does,' said Fern, 'I just do,' said Sam.

'Well it seems weird to me,' said Kate 'but weird stuff seems to happen when I'm with you, Fern. My name is Kate,' she said smiling at Sam.

'I'm pleased to meet you, Kate. I didn't see you after the second half of the concert,' Sam said to Fern 'what did you …' he hesitated and had an anxious look on his face.

'The music?' Fern prompted 'What did I think of the music? Is that what you were going to ask?'

'Yes,' he said, still looking worried.

'I thought it was great, I really enjoyed it.'

His face lit up in a huge smile. 'Really? You're not just ...' his voice trailed off into silence.

'Saying that?' She laughed 'I hope you don't mind me finishing your sentences for you?'

'No,' he laughed. 'The music, anything else?' he prompted her.

'I thought it went really well with the words. It was like you could actually hear the Native Indians stomping round a camp fire, dum, dum dum' she stamped her feet 'dum, dum dum.' Kate and Sam joined in the stamping. 'And the words,' she went on, 'I read the poem afterwards "by the shores of Gitchee Gumee, by the shining big sea water" has a lovely kind of up and downness. Sorry, that probably isn't a proper word but I can't think how else to describe it.'

'I'd probably call that "rhythm"', said Sam.

'OK,' said Fern 'the words had a lovely up and down rhythm and the music fitted really well.'

'So that means the people in the poem lived by the sea, right?' said Kate 'that's what "big sea water" means?'

'Well, actually, I think it's a lake,' Sam said 'Lake Superior. It's a huge lake, bigger than a lot of seas. Gitchee Gumee is what the Native Indians called it. If you lived beside Lake Superior it would probably feel like living beside the sea.'

'And I got a feather from one of the headdresses, see.' She took it out of her pocket and held it up but, before he could say anything, she heard her Mother's voice.

'Fern! Kate!'

'Oh no, that's my Mum. We're going to have to go, Sam.'

'I know,' said Sam, sadly 'maybe I'll see you again Fern and Kate,' he held out his hand and they each shook it.

'Coming Mum,' Fern called.

'What have you been doing? How long does it take to take a picture and what were you doing in the garden? You really shouldn't have been in there, it's private property.'

'Sorry Mum, we thought we saw something in the hedge.'

'So you thought you'd go in and look? That was really silly, you should have stayed on the path, whatever will you get up to next, Fern. You're a sensible girl Kate, why didn't you stop her?'

Kate didn't really think she was expected to answer and she couldn't really think of anything to say so she just shrugged.

'Well anyway, did you get your pictures?'

'Yes thanks, Mum.'

'In that case we should go and catch the bus home. Will you stay with us for tea, Kate?'

'Oh, yes please, I'd really like that. Thanks ever so much Mrs Green.'

The Bandon Hill cemetery wasn't as Fern had imagined it. There was no shining lake surrounded by trees like in the Wedding Feast poem. It had been silly to think there might be she realised, this was Croydon, there were no lakes in Croydon, well not proper ones anyway.

She had never been to a cemetery before, she felt just a little bit scared and held her Mother's hand quite tightly. Kate hadn't wanted to come with them. 'I don't know why you'd want to go to a cemetery, Fern,' she had said 'it'll be full of dead people and,' she added 'there might be ghosts.' She had shuddered visibly at the thought of it. Fern wasn't very happy about meeting any ghosts but she badly wanted to see where her friend Samuel had ended up. She knew he was dead and she tried to tell herself that it didn't really matter but, deep down, she wanted to make sure the grave was being looked after properly, he deserved that she thought.

They found Samuel Coleridge-Taylor's grave after a bit of hunting around, 'I hope I don't meet him here,' she thought. In fact she must have said it out loud without realising because her Mother said 'he's dead, you do understand that don't you, Fern?' She nodded. 'I just want to …'. Her voice trailed off because, now that they were here, she wasn't really sure what she wanted to do.

'Well,' her Mother said 'it's nice to see that it's being looked after. Someone obviously left some flowers a while ago though they're past their best now. We can replace them with the daffodils we brought.'

Fern bent down and carefully arranged the flowers in front of the tombstone. Her Mother read the inscription softly:

""Too young to die
his great simplicity
his happy courage
in an alien world

his gentleness
made all that knew him
love him.'"

'That's beautiful,' said Fern, dabbing away a
tear that was rolling down her cheek.

'It is,' said her Mother, thoughtfully, 'very nice,
very moving.' They held hands for a few
moments.

A chilly breeze suddenly rattled through the
leaves of the nearby trees. 'Come on, Fern, we
should go now, it looks as if it's going to rain
and we'll get soaked out here in the open.'

'OK, Mum, I just wanted to see his grave.'
Then she remembered one more thing that she
had brought with her. She knelt down, pulled
the feather out of her coat pocket and tucked it
into the vase along with the daffodils. 'Just so
that he knows I came,' she said.

Her Mother gave her a worried look 'you do
say the strangest things sometimes, Fern,' she
paused 'but it's a nice thought.' The first drops

of rain started to fall in big splodges. 'We'd better hurry, Fern.'

They turned and left, not noticing the small boy who had been watching them from behind a tree. He bent down, pulled a violin out of its battered case and started to play. He closed his eyes, lost in the beauty of the sad melody he was playing. The feather fluttered gently in the breeze as the rain started to fall more heavily.

At the cemetery gates Fern's Mother pointed up at the sky 'a rainbow,' she said. The sun had come out from behind a cloud and a colourful arc was forming over the cemetery.

'It's beautiful' Fern said 'I'm glad we came.'

*

'That was a lovely "show and tell", Fern,' said Mrs Grainger 'thank you for sharing that with the class. I'll give you a merit sticker for that, your first I think. Excellent work.'

Fern beamed, feeling really happy and Kate led the class in a little burst of applause.

'You often surprise me Fern, sometimes it's in a good way, like a rainbow on a cloudy day.'

'Thank you Miss.'

The Life and Times of Samuel Coleridge-Taylor

Samuel Coleridge Taylor was born on 15th August 1875 in Holborn which is in Central London. Later in life he chose to put a hyphen (the little line) between his last two names but that isn't how his name was written when he was a child.

Samuel's Father

His Father was Daniel Taylor. Daniel was originally from Freetown in Sierra Leone which is on the West coast of the African continent. He was probably born in 1849, the son of a wealthy Nigerian merchant who had made Freetown his home.

Daniel went to school in Freetown and must have done well because in 1869, at the age of 20, he was sent to England to continue his education. He went first to a college in Taunton in the West of England and in 1873 he got a place to study medicine at the medical school at Kings College Hospital in London. He completed his studies in 1874 and graduated. He must have been very clever to successfully become a Doctor so quickly.

He may have worked in London assisting another Doctor for a short time and we think he may have met Samuel's mother while doing that.

Samuel's Mother

Samuel's Mother was definitely called Alice but no one is quite sure what her family name (surname) was. Samuel's birth certificate shows his Mother's name as 'Alice Taylor' but in fact Alice almost certainly never married Dr Taylor so she may have used the name to pretend she was married. At that time, for a child to be born to unmarried parents was definitely frowned upon.

The relationship between Alice and Daniel didn't last very long because we know that by

November 1875 Daniel was working in Sierra Leone.

Samuel's childhood

It's quite likely that Dr Taylor had left England by the time his son was born (in fact, he may not even have known Alice was going to have a baby) so she would have to bring the child up without his help. We must assume that it was Alice who chose her son's names: Samuel Coleridge. Perhaps she had a keen interest in poetry because the names echo those of Samuel Taylor Coleridge who was a very popular poet at the time.

Fortunately Alice wasn't completely alone with the baby as she continued to live in Holborn with the people who were probably (we can't be quite sure) her parents (there are quite good reasons to believe that they weren't married either).

All the evidence suggests this was a loving home for young Samuel even though his Father was absent.

In about 1877, when Samuel would have been two, Alice and her family moved out of Holborn and went to live in Croydon, on the southern edge of London.

At some point in the early 1880s Alice met and married a man called George Evans. Alice's family were not rich and neither was Mr Evans but he did have a steady income from his job working for the railway company. He also showed some courage in marrying a lady who was the single Mother of a mixed race child at a time when there would have been very few such children in Croydon.

Samuel went to a school in Tamworth Road, Croydon. We don't know exactly when he started going there but we do know he was there by December 1885 when he would have been ten. We also know that he was the only non-white boy, not just in his class but in the whole school. Although this class photo is a bit blurry you can see him at the right hand end of the second row from the front.

1. Class photograph, the British School, Tamworth Road, Croydon

There can't be much doubt that he was picked on and bullied. In later life he told how some boys tried to set fire to his curly hair just to see if it would burn – a horrible thing to do.

We know one other thing about young Samuel, he was a very talented musician from an early age.

Samuel's early interest in music

Alice was quite musical and, in spite of not having a lot of money, we know that she and

Mr Evans had a piano in their house. There's evidence that Alice's parents were musical too.

Clearly they passed that on to Samuel because at an early age he started to learn the violin. Soon he was playing the tune of the National Anthem on his violin while the rest of the children at school sang the words. He also won a singing competition at the school.

By the time he was eleven he was playing his violin in concerts outside the school in Croydon and composing his own tunes to play on it.

But his musical career might not have got any further if it hadn't been for a piece of good luck.

A lucky break

At the time Samuel was young, people with a lot of money were encouraged to help people who were less well off. There is a story that, on his way home from school one day, with his violin tucked under his arm, young Samuel stopped to play a game of marbles. It just happened to be outside the house of a man called Joseph Beckwith. Joseph was a professional musician who conducted a local orchestra and just happened to be a violin teacher. Mr Beckwith was at home and was intrigued by the boy playing outside his house and particularly by the violin the boy was carrying.

Although it may not be strictly true, It's a nice story. But what is true is that Mr Beckwith became Samuel's violin teacher for the next seven years.

This is a rather smart violin, the one Samuel played as a child was probably a little bit more battered than this one:

One of the Governor's at Samuel's school, Colonel Herbert Walters, also recognised the talent that Samuel had and helped him whenever he could.

The Royal College of Music

Encouraged by Walters and Beckwith, Samuel was able to get a place at the Royal College of Music. He was only fifteen when he first went there in 1890, younger than most of the other students. Younger, with darker skin and very shy, Samuel must have found it a very difficult experience but he stuck at it.

He worked hard for almost seven years at the Royal College, learning the piano, continuing to play the violin and, crucially, learning how to compose music.

He was twenty two when he left the College and had already composed a lot of music and had some of it published and performed.

Marriage and family

After leaving college, Samuel was living with his family at Dagnall Park (the house Fern and Kate visited in the story) and working on what was to become his most famous composition, 'Hiawatha's Wedding Feast'.

It was first performed at his old college in November 1898 and it was a great success. One person who heard it described it as 'fresh and original'.

Samuel married a girl, Jessie Walmsley, who had also been to the Royal College. She was a few years older than him and completed her studies there in 1893 when Samuel was only eighteen. They may have known each other at college but they probably became friends at musical events in Croydon, where Jessie also lived.

In December 1899 Samuel and Jesse married at Holy Trinity church in Selhurst. The church isn't there anymore but a war memorial stands where the church used to be.

There isn't much doubt that Jessie's parents disapproved of their daughter marrying Samuel because of his colour although they did, probably reluctantly, attend the wedding ceremony.

Samuel and his wife had two children, a son in 1900 who was named Hiawatha and a daughter,

Gwendolyn (she later changed her name to Avril), born in 1903.

Hiawatha

The music that Fern and Kate heard performed was 'Hiawatha's Wedding Feast'. This was Samuel's most popular composition while he was alive. It was so popular that he wrote two more parts: 'the Death of Minniehaha' (in 1899); and 'Hiawatha's Departure' (in 1900).

'Hiawatha' was very popular and people often dressed up as Native Indians (sometimes also called Red Indians) to go to performances. This is the sort of headdress that they might have worn and that Fern and Kate might have seen in the concert at the Fairfield Halls.

Although he composed many other pieces of music, some of it very good, 'Hiawatha' is still his best known work today. In terms of popularity, he never quite reached the same heights again.

Later life

Making a living out of composing music has never been easy and most composers have to make extra money where they can by teaching or judging music competitions. He was also in demand as a conductor, the person who helps an orchestra or choir play together as a team rather than as individuals.

He did make enough to live on but he was never rich. The next picture shows him when he was a successful composer.

We can't be certain but some of the pictures you can see on top of the piano are probably of his wife and children and, perhaps, his Mother. One of them is also thought to be of one of his teachers at the Royal College of Music. It's also interesting that there are tall candles attached to the piano and an oil lamp resting on top of it. In those days houses didn't have electric lights so he would have composed his music and played the piano by the light of these candles and the oil lamp. As Fern discovered in the story, they didn't have electric guitars either, these were first made about forty years after Samuel Coleridge-Taylor had died.

He travelled a lot and had to work very hard, complaining more than once in letters that he was 'tired' or should cut back on his work load a bit. But he never really did cut back and on 28th August 1912 he was taken ill on his way to West Croydon train station. The weather had been unusually wet and cold that month and, worn out by all the hard work, he had caught something called 'pneumonia'. Now, with modern medicine, he would probably have recovered but, on 1st September he died with his wife and mother at his bedside.

Crowds lined the streets 'three or four deep' to pay their respects as he was taken to his final resting place at Bandon Hill cemetery in Croydon.

The writing that Fern's Mother reads out in the story is on the gravestone.

In many ways the story of Samuel's life might seem like a sad one, he died at a young age, leaving behind a widow and two small children.

But he achieved a great deal in his short life, overcoming the many obstacles he faced, and writing music that is still appreciated by many people over a hundred years later.

Samuel Coleridge Taylor had a good life and will be remembered fondly, as the words on the gravestone say 'He lives while music lives'.

Thank you

Photographs:

- photo of Fairfield Halls, Croydon, and of the plaque on the wall, by kind permission of James Spring on behalf of Fairfield Halls
- thanks to Lindsay Ould and the team at the Croydon Archive for tracing the two photos of Samuel Coleridge Taylor as an adult and giving permission to use them.
- The school photo on page 29 was in a book written by Geoffrey Self ('The Hiawatha Man'). The book is out of print now and Geoffrey Self died several years ago so I have not been able to trace the owner of the image.

Most of the biographical information is available on Wikipedia but I checked for accuracy against:

The Hiawatha Man' by Geoffrey Self and 'Coleridge-Taylor – A Centenary Celebration' by Jeff Green.

Also thanks to Sean Creighton for organising a fascinating walking tour of some of the houses where Coleridge-Taylor lived in the Selhurst area.

The author is a member of 'The Clerkenwell Writers Asylum' and the support of my fellow members is much appreciated.

<u>Other titles in this series</u>

'Fern and Kate meet Dido Elizabeth Belle'

<u>Planned titles</u>

'Fern and Kate meet Walter Tull'

'Fern and Kate meet Mary Seacole'

<u>Feedback</u>

Feedback on this booklet is welcome at:
dgleave1937@gmail.com

13281112R00032

Printed in Great Britain
by Amazon.co.uk, Ltd.,
Marston Gate.